STAR WARS

EPISODE VI
RETURN OF THE JEDI

VOLUME ONE

Script
ARCHIE GOODWIN

Art
AL WILLIAMSON
CARLOS GARZÓN

Colors
CARY PORTER
PERRY McNAMEE

Lettering
ED KING

Cover Art
BILL SIENKIEWICZ

DARK
HORSE
COMICS

Spotlight

VISIT US AT
www.abdopublishing.com

Reinforced library bound edition published in 2010 by Spotlight, a division of the ABDO Group, 8000 West 78th Street, Edina, Minnesota 55439. Spotlight produces high-quality reinforced library bound editions for schools and libraries. Published by agreement with Dark Horse Comics, Inc., and Lucasfilm Ltd.

Printed in the United States of America, Melrose Park, Illinois.
092009
012010

 PRINTED ON RECYCLED PAPER

Library of Congress Cataloging-in-Publication Data

Goodwin, Archie.
  Episode VI : return of the Jedi / based on the screenplay by George Lucas ; script adaptation Archie Goodwin ; artists Al Williamson & Carlos Garzon ; letterer Ed King. -- Reinforced library bound ed.
       p. cm. -- (Star wars)
  "Dark Horse Comics."
  ISBN 978-1-59961-705-3 (vol. 1) -- ISBN 978-1-59961-706-0 (vol. 2) -- ISBN 978-1-59961-707-7 (vol. 3) -- ISBN 978-1-59961-708-4 (vol. 4)
  1. Graphic novels. [1. Graphic novels.] I. Lucas, George, 1944- II. Williamson, Al, 1931- III. Garzon, Carlos. IV. Return of the Jedi (Motion picture) V. Title. VI. Title: Episode six. VII. Title: Return of the Jedi.
  PZ7.7.G656Epk 2010
  [Fic]--dc22
                               2009030862

All Spotlight books have reinforced library bindings and are manufactured in the United States of America.

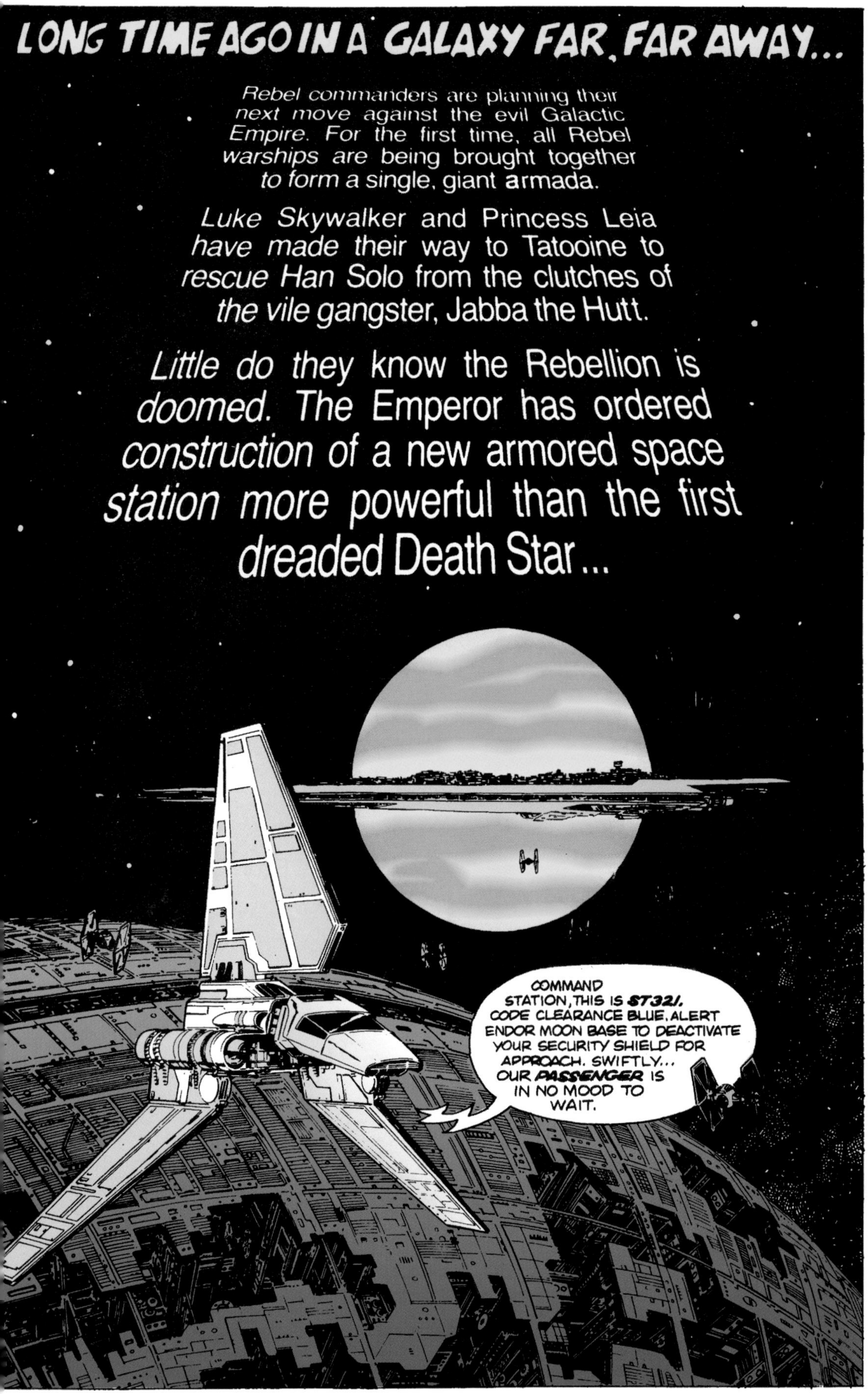
LONG TIME AGO IN A GALAXY FAR, FAR AWAY...
Rebel commanders are planning their next move against the evil Galactic Empire. For the first time, all Rebel warships are being brought together to form a single, giant armada.
Luke Skywalker and Princess Leia have made their way to Tatooine to rescue Han Solo from the clutches of the vile gangster, Jabba the Hutt.
Little do they know the Rebellion is doomed. The Emperor has ordered construction of a new armored space station more powerful than the first dreaded Death Star...
COMMAND STATION, THIS IS ST321. CODE CLEARANCE BLUE. ALERT ENDOR MOON BASE TO DEACTIVATE YOUR SECURITY SHIELD FOR APPROACH. SWIFTLY... OUR PASSENGER IS IN NO MOOD TO WAIT.

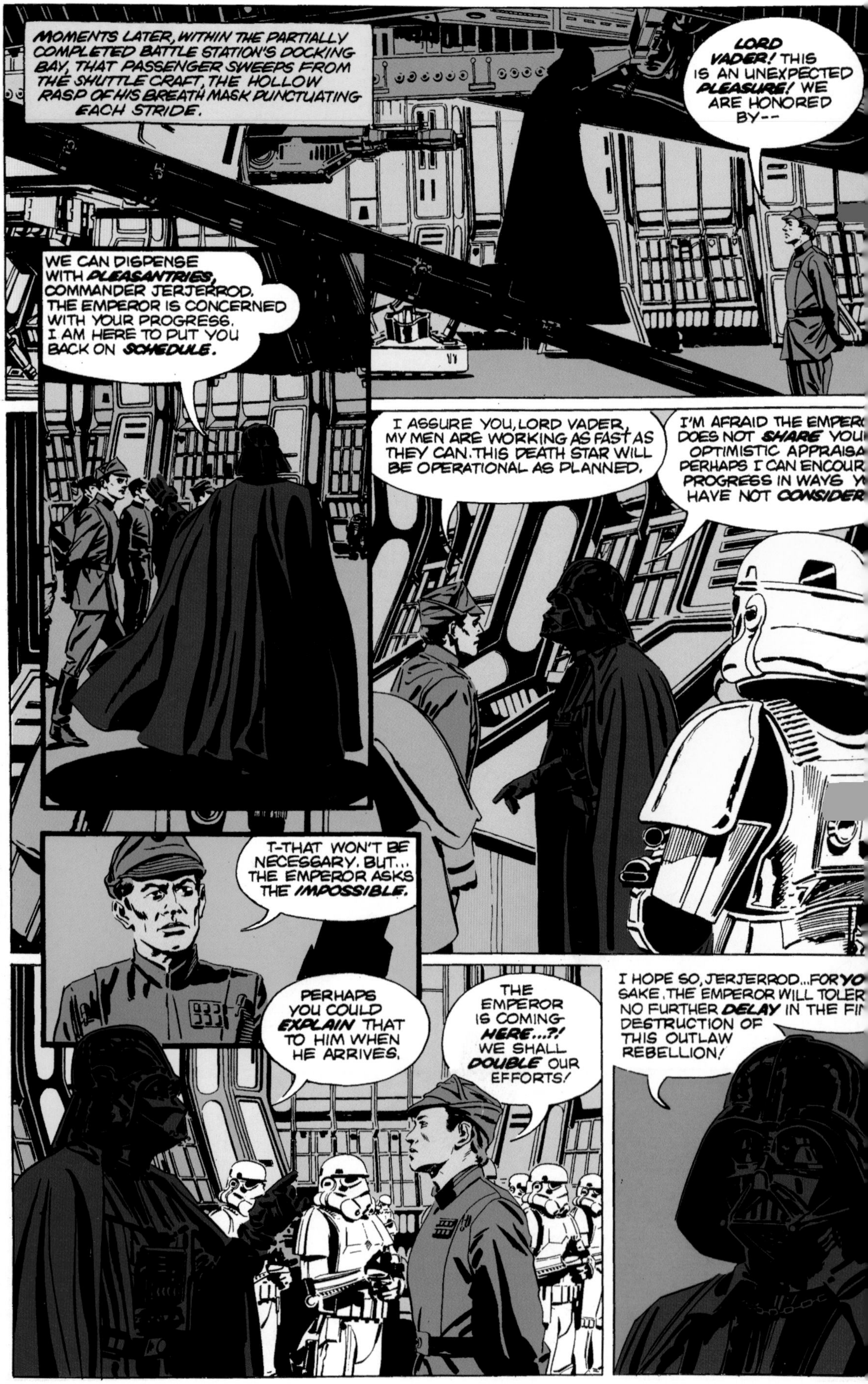
MOMENTS LATER, WITHIN THE PARTIALLY COMPLETED BATTLE STATION'S DOCKING BAY, THAT PASSENGER SWEEPS FROM THE SHUTTLE CRAFT, THE HOLLOW RASP OF HIS BREATH MASK PUNCTUATING EACH STRIDE.
LORD VADER! THIS IS AN UNEXPECTED PLEASURE! WE ARE HONORED BY--
WE CAN DISPENSE WITH PLEASANTRIES, COMMANDER JERJERROD. THE EMPEROR IS CONCERNED WITH YOUR PROGRESS. I AM HERE TO PUT YOU BACK ON SCHEDULE.
I ASSURE YOU, LORD VADER, MY MEN ARE WORKING AS FAST AS THEY CAN. THIS DEATH STAR WILL BE OPERATIONAL AS PLANNED.
I'M AFRAID THE EMPER DOES NOT SHARE YOU OPTIMISTIC APPRAISA PERHAPS I CAN ENCOUR PROGRESS IN WAYS Y HAVE NOT CONSIDER
T-THAT WON'T BE NECESSARY. BUT... THE EMPEROR ASKS THE IMPOSSIBLE.
PERHAPS YOU COULD EXPLAIN THAT TO HIM WHEN HE ARRIVES.
THE EMPEROR IS COMING HERE...?! WE SHALL DOUBLE OUR EFFORTS!
I HOPE SO, JERJERROD...FOR YO SAKE. THE EMPEROR WILL TOLER NO FURTHER DELAY IN THE FI DESTRUCTION OF THIS OUTLAW REBELLION!

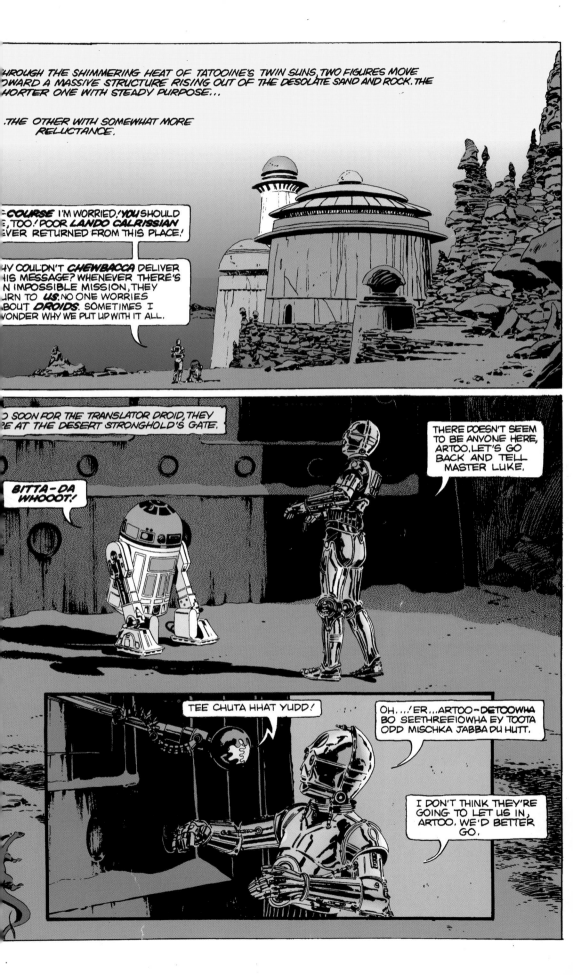

THROUGH THE SHIMMERING HEAT OF TATOOINE'S TWIN SUNS, TWO FIGURES MOVE TOWARD A MASSIVE STRUCTURE RISING OUT OF THE DESOLATE SAND AND ROCK. THE SHORTER ONE WITH STEADY PURPOSE...

...THE OTHER WITH SOMEWHAT MORE RELUCTANCE.

OF *COURSE* I'M WORRIED! *YOU* SHOULD BE, TOO! POOR *LANDO CALRISSIAN* NEVER RETURNED FROM THIS PLACE!

WHY COULDN'T *CHEWBACCA* DELIVER THIS MESSAGE? WHENEVER THERE'S AN IMPOSSIBLE MISSION, THEY TURN TO *US*. NO ONE WORRIES ABOUT *DROIDS*. SOMETIMES I WONDER WHY WE PUT UP WITH IT ALL.

TOO SOON FOR THE TRANSLATOR DROID, THEY ARE AT THE DESERT STRONGHOLD'S GATE.

BITTA—DA WHOOOT!

THERE DOESN'T SEEM TO BE ANYONE HERE, ARTOO. LET'S GO BACK AND TELL MASTER LUKE.

TEE CHUTA HHAT YUDD!

OH....'ER...ARTOO—DETOOWHA BO SEETHREEIOWHA EY TOOTA ODD MISCHKA JABBA DU HUTT.

I DON'T THINK THEY'RE GOING TO LET US IN, ARTOO. WE'D BETTER GO.

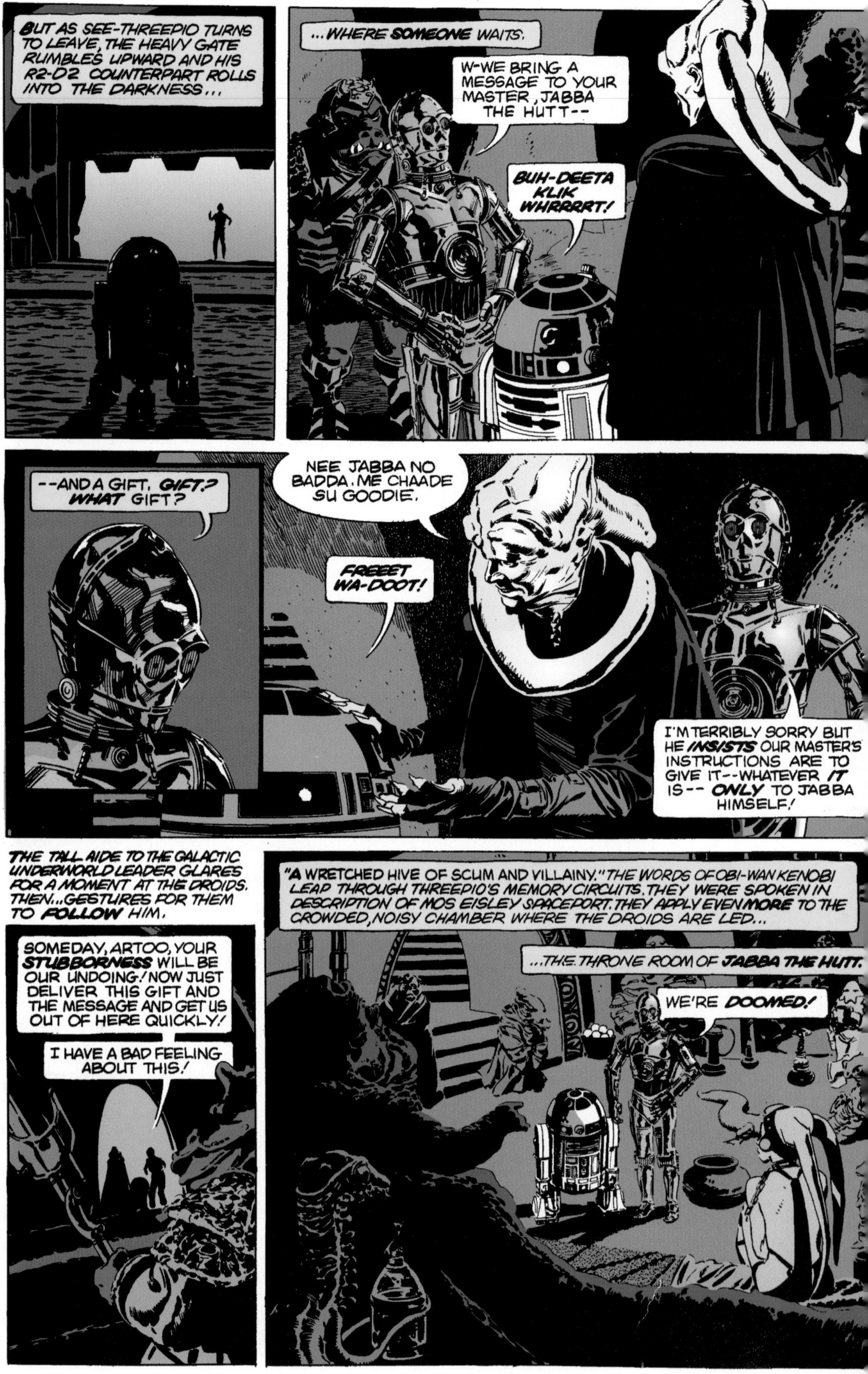
BUT AS SEE-THREEPIO TURNS TO LEAVE, THE HEAVY GATE RUMBLES UPWARD AND HIS R2-D2 COUNTERPART ROLLS INTO THE DARKNESS...
...WHERE SOMEONE WAITS.
W-WE BRING A MESSAGE TO YOUR MASTER, JABBA THE HUTT--
BUH-DEETA KLIK WHRRRRT!
--AND A GIFT. GIFT? WHAT GIFT?
NEE JABBA NO BADDA. ME CHAADE SU GOODIE.
FREEET WA-DOOT!
I'M TERRIBLY SORRY BUT HE INSISTS OUR MASTER'S INSTRUCTIONS ARE TO GIVE IT--WHATEVER IT IS-- ONLY TO JABBA HIMSELF!
THE TALL AIDE TO THE GALACTIC UNDERWORLD LEADER GLARES FOR A MOMENT AT THE DROIDS. THEN...GESTURES FOR THEM TO FOLLOW HIM.
SOMEDAY, ARTOO, YOUR STUBBORNESS WILL BE OUR UNDOING! NOW JUST DELIVER THIS GIFT AND THE MESSAGE AND GET US OUT OF HERE QUICKLY!
I HAVE A BAD FEELING ABOUT THIS!
"A WRETCHED HIVE OF SCUM AND VILLAINY." THE WORDS OF OBI-WAN KENOBI LEAP THROUGH THREEPIO'S MEMORY CIRCUITS. THEY WERE SPOKEN IN DESCRIPTION OF MOS EISLEY SPACEPORT. THEY APPLY EVEN MORE TO THE CROWDED, NOISY CHAMBER WHERE THE DROIDS ARE LED...
...THE THRONE ROOM OF JABBA THE HUTT.
WE'RE DOOMED!

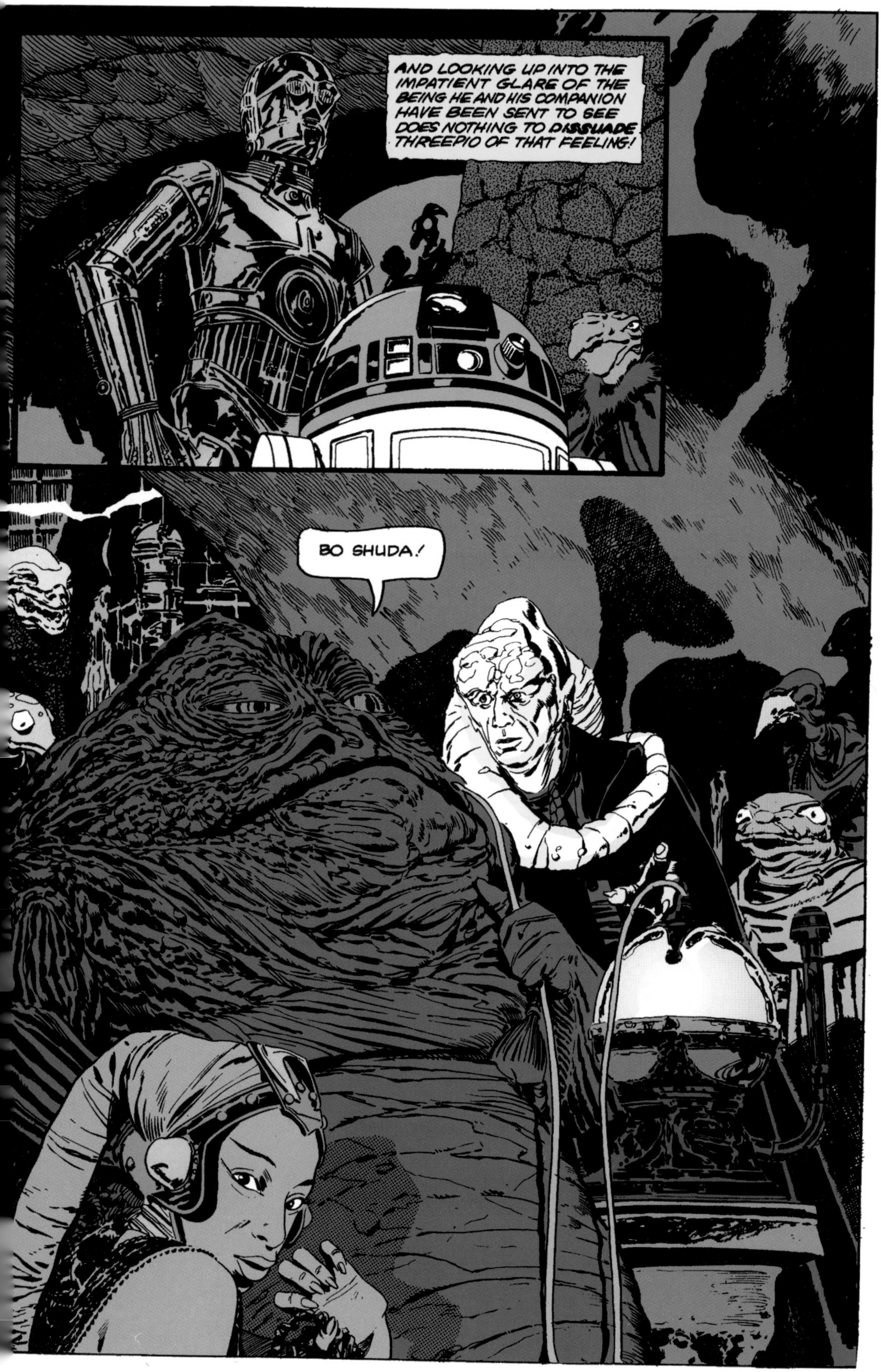
AND LOOKING UP INTO THE IMPATIENT GLARE OF THE BEING HE AND HIS COMPANION HAVE BEEN SENT TO SEE DOES NOTHING TO DISSUADE THREEPIO OF THAT FEELING!
BO SHUDA!

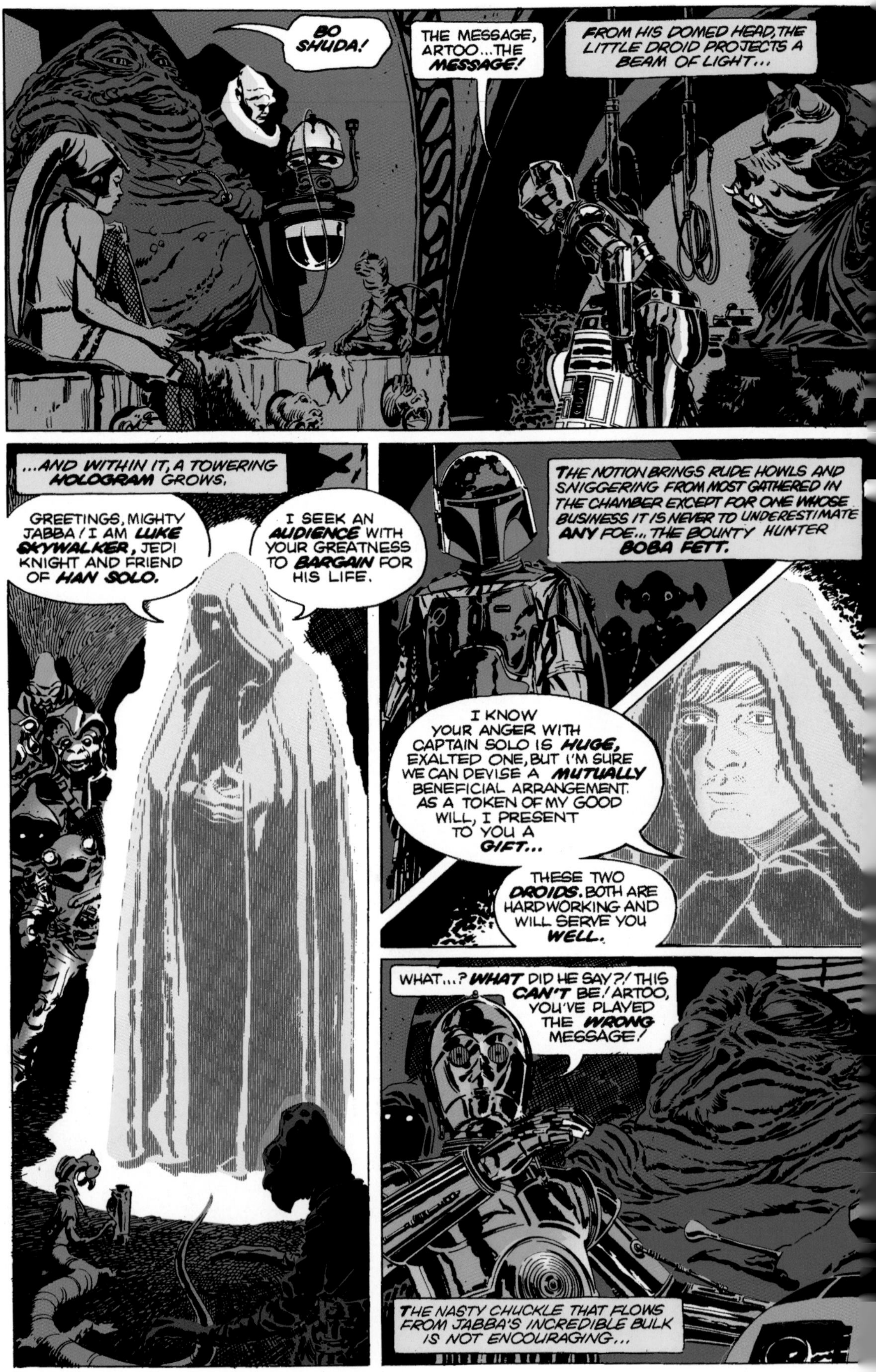
BO SHUDA!
THE MESSAGE, ARTOO...THE MESSAGE!
FROM HIS DOMED HEAD, THE LITTLE DROID PROJECTS A BEAM OF LIGHT...
...AND WITHIN IT, A TOWERING HOLOGRAM GROWS.
GREETINGS, MIGHTY JABBA! I AM LUKE SKYWALKER, JEDI KNIGHT AND FRIEND OF HAN SOLO.
I SEEK AN AUDIENCE WITH YOUR GREATNESS TO BARGAIN FOR HIS LIFE.
THE NOTION BRINGS RUDE HOWLS AND SNIGGERING FROM MOST GATHERED IN THE CHAMBER EXCEPT FOR ONE WHOSE BUSINESS IT IS NEVER TO UNDERESTIMATE ANY FOE... THE BOUNTY HUNTER BOBA FETT.
I KNOW YOUR ANGER WITH CAPTAIN SOLO IS HUGE, EXALTED ONE, BUT I'M SURE WE CAN DEVISE A MUTUALLY BENEFICIAL ARRANGEMENT. AS A TOKEN OF MY GOOD WILL, I PRESENT TO YOU A GIFT...
THESE TWO DROIDS. BOTH ARE HARDWORKING AND WILL SERVE YOU WELL.
WHAT...? WHAT DID HE SAY?! THIS CAN'T BE! ARTOO, YOU'VE PLAYED THE WRONG MESSAGE!
THE NASTY CHUCKLE THAT FLOWS FROM JABBA'S INCREDIBLE BULK IS NOT ENCOURAGING...

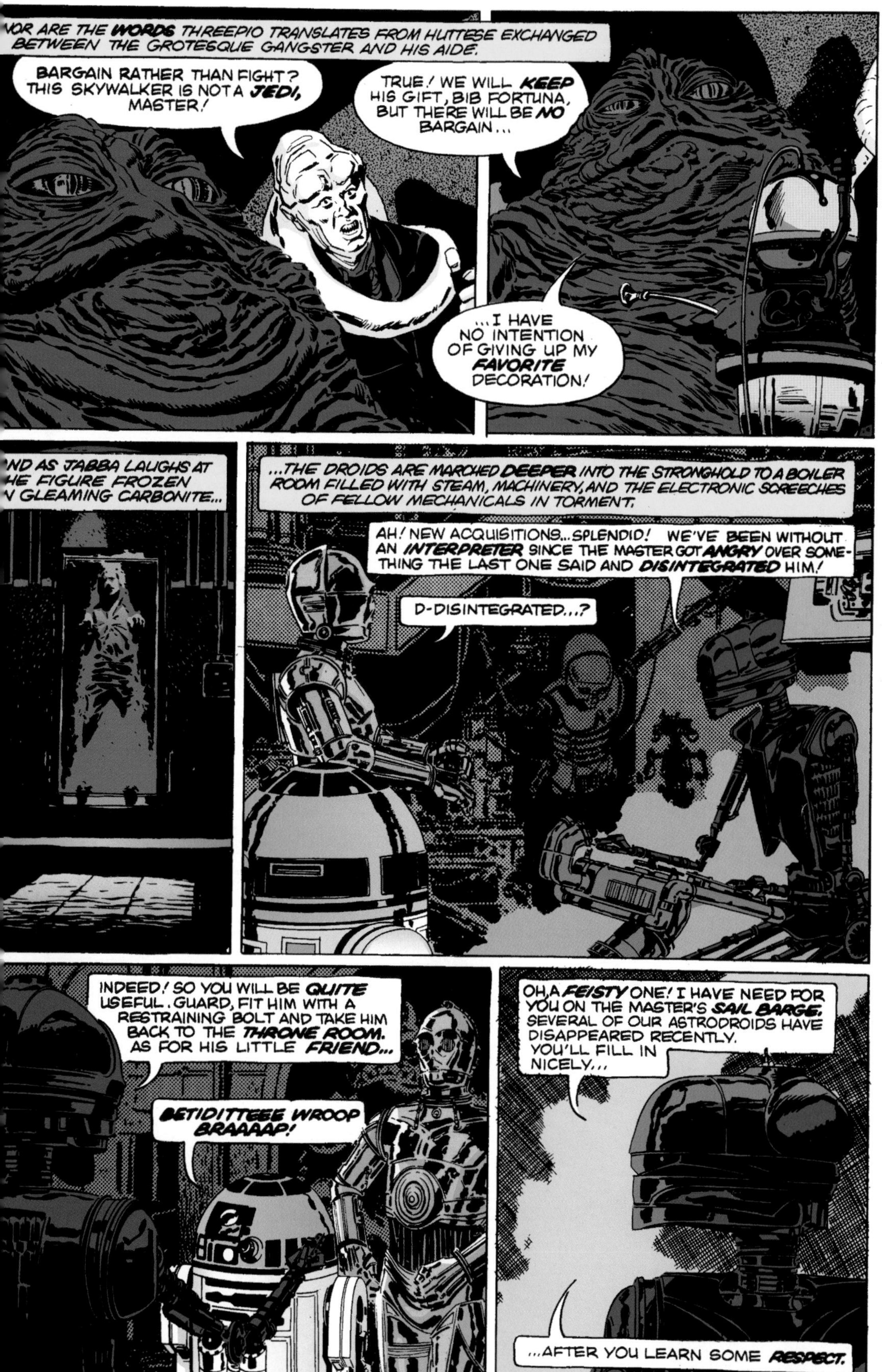

NOR ARE THE WORDS THREEPIO TRANSLATES FROM HUTTESE EXCHANGED BETWEEN THE GROTESQUE GANGSTER AND HIS AIDE.
BARGAIN RATHER THAN FIGHT? THIS SKYWALKER IS NOT A JEDI, MASTER!
TRUE! WE WILL KEEP HIS GIFT, BIB FORTUNA, BUT THERE WILL BE NO BARGAIN...
...I HAVE NO INTENTION OF GIVING UP MY FAVORITE DECORATION!
ND AS JABBA LAUGHS AT HE FIGURE FROZEN N GLEAMING CARBONITE...
...THE DROIDS ARE MARCHED DEEPER INTO THE STRONGHOLD TO A BOILER ROOM FILLED WITH STEAM, MACHINERY, AND THE ELECTRONIC SCREECHES OF FELLOW MECHANICALS IN TORMENT.
AH! NEW ACQUISITIONS...SPLENDID! WE'VE BEEN WITHOUT AN INTERPRETER SINCE THE MASTER GOT ANGRY OVER SOMETHING THE LAST ONE SAID AND DISINTEGRATED HIM!
D-DISINTEGRATED...?
INDEED! SO YOU WILL BE QUITE USEFUL. GUARD, FIT HIM WITH A RESTRAINING BOLT AND TAKE HIM BACK TO THE THRONE ROOM. AS FOR HIS LITTLE FRIEND...
BETIDITTEEE WROOP BRAAAAP!
OH, A FEISTY ONE! I HAVE NEED FOR YOU ON THE MASTER'S SAIL BARGE. SEVERAL OF OUR ASTRODROIDS HAVE DISAPPEARED RECENTLY. YOU'LL FILL IN NICELY...
...AFTER YOU LEARN SOME RESPECT.

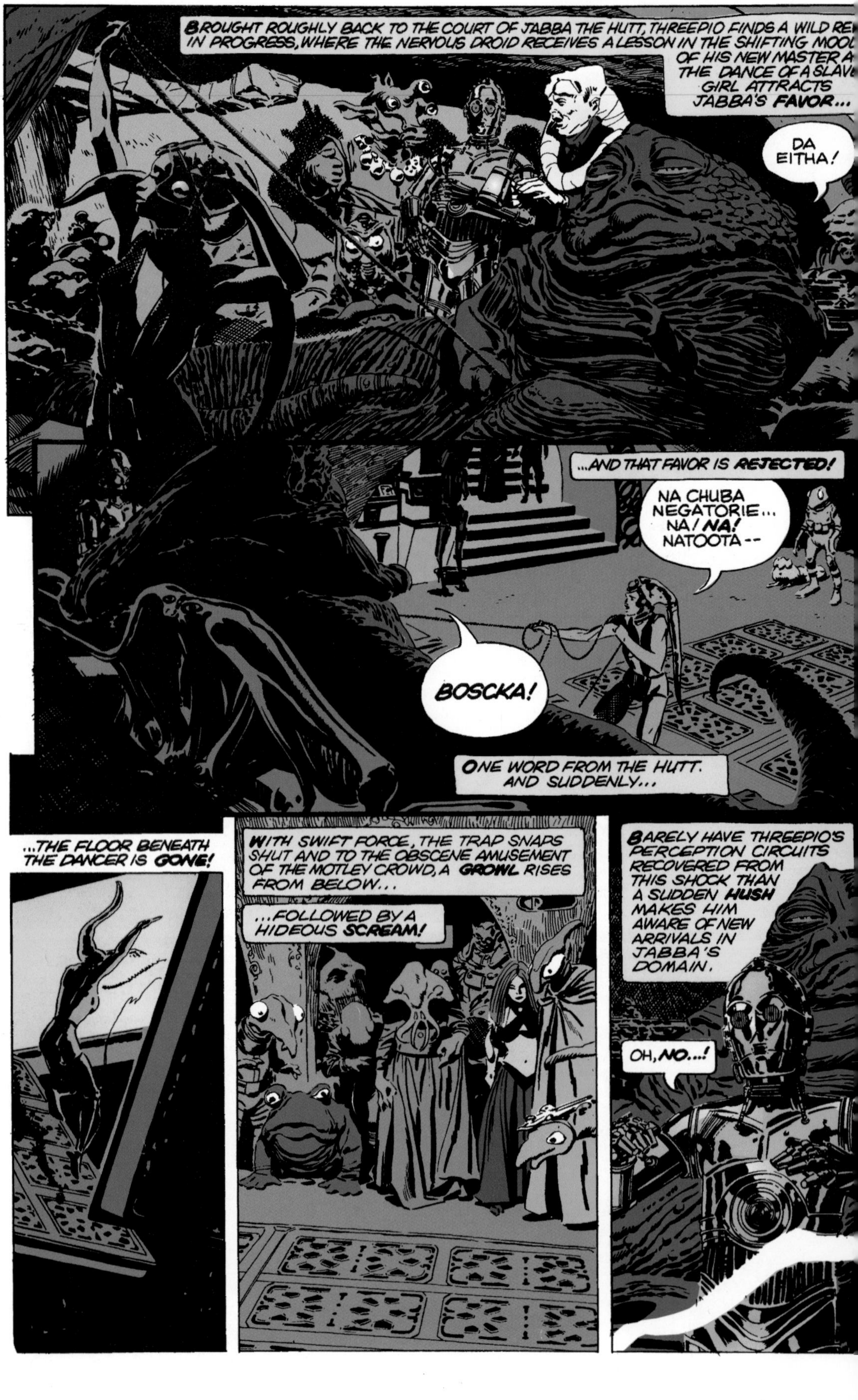
BROUGHT ROUGHLY BACK TO THE COURT OF JABBA THE HUTT, THREEPIO FINDS A WILD RE IN PROGRESS, WHERE THE NERVOUS DROID RECEIVES A LESSON IN THE SHIFTING MOOD OF HIS NEW MASTER A THE DANCE OF A SLAVE GIRL ATTRACTS JABBA'S FAVOR...
DA EITHA!
...AND THAT FAVOR IS REJECTED!
NA CHUBA NEGATORIE... NA! NA! NATOOTA--
BOSCKA!
ONE WORD FROM THE HUTT. AND SUDDENLY...
...THE FLOOR BENEATH THE DANCER IS GONE!
WITH SWIFT FORCE, THE TRAP SNAPS SHUT AND TO THE OBSCENE AMUSEMENT OF THE MOTLEY CROWD, A GROWL RISES FROM BELOW...
...FOLLOWED BY A HIDEOUS SCREAM!
BARELY HAVE THREEPIO'S PERCEPTION CIRCUITS RECOVERED FROM THIS SHOCK THAN A SUDDEN HUSH MAKES HIM AWARE OF NEW ARRIVALS IN JABBA'S DOMAIN.
OH, NO...!

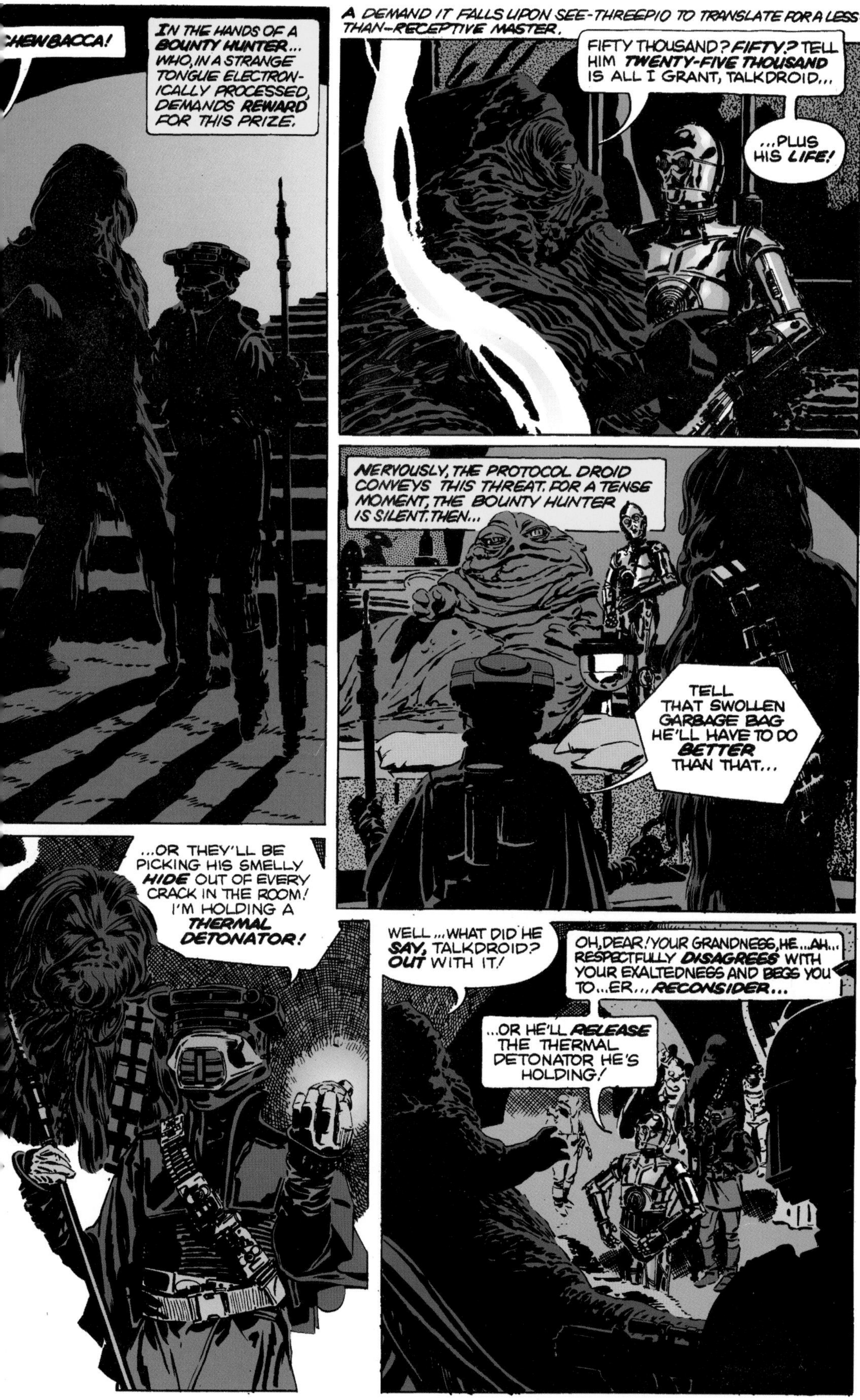
CHEWBACCA!
IN THE HANDS OF A BOUNTY HUNTER... WHO, IN A STRANGE TONGUE ELECTRONICALLY PROCESSED, DEMANDS REWARD FOR THIS PRIZE.
A DEMAND IT FALLS UPON SEE-THREEPIO TO TRANSLATE FOR A LESS-THAN-RECEPTIVE MASTER.
FIFTY THOUSAND? FIFTY? TELL HIM TWENTY-FIVE THOUSAND IS ALL I GRANT, TALKDROID...
...PLUS HIS LIFE!
NERVOUSLY, THE PROTOCOL DROID CONVEYS THIS THREAT. FOR A TENSE MOMENT, THE BOUNTY HUNTER IS SILENT. THEN...
TELL THAT SWOLLEN GARBAGE BAG HE'LL HAVE TO DO BETTER THAN THAT...
...OR THEY'LL BE PICKING HIS SMELLY HIDE OUT OF EVERY CRACK IN THE ROOM! I'M HOLDING A THERMAL DETONATOR!
WELL...WHAT DID HE SAY, TALKDROID? OUT WITH IT!
OH, DEAR! YOUR GRANDNESS, HE...AH... RESPECTFULLY DISAGREES WITH YOUR EXALTEDNESS AND BEGS YOU TO...ER... RECONSIDER...
...OR HE'LL RELEASE THE THERMAL DETONATOR HE'S HOLDING!

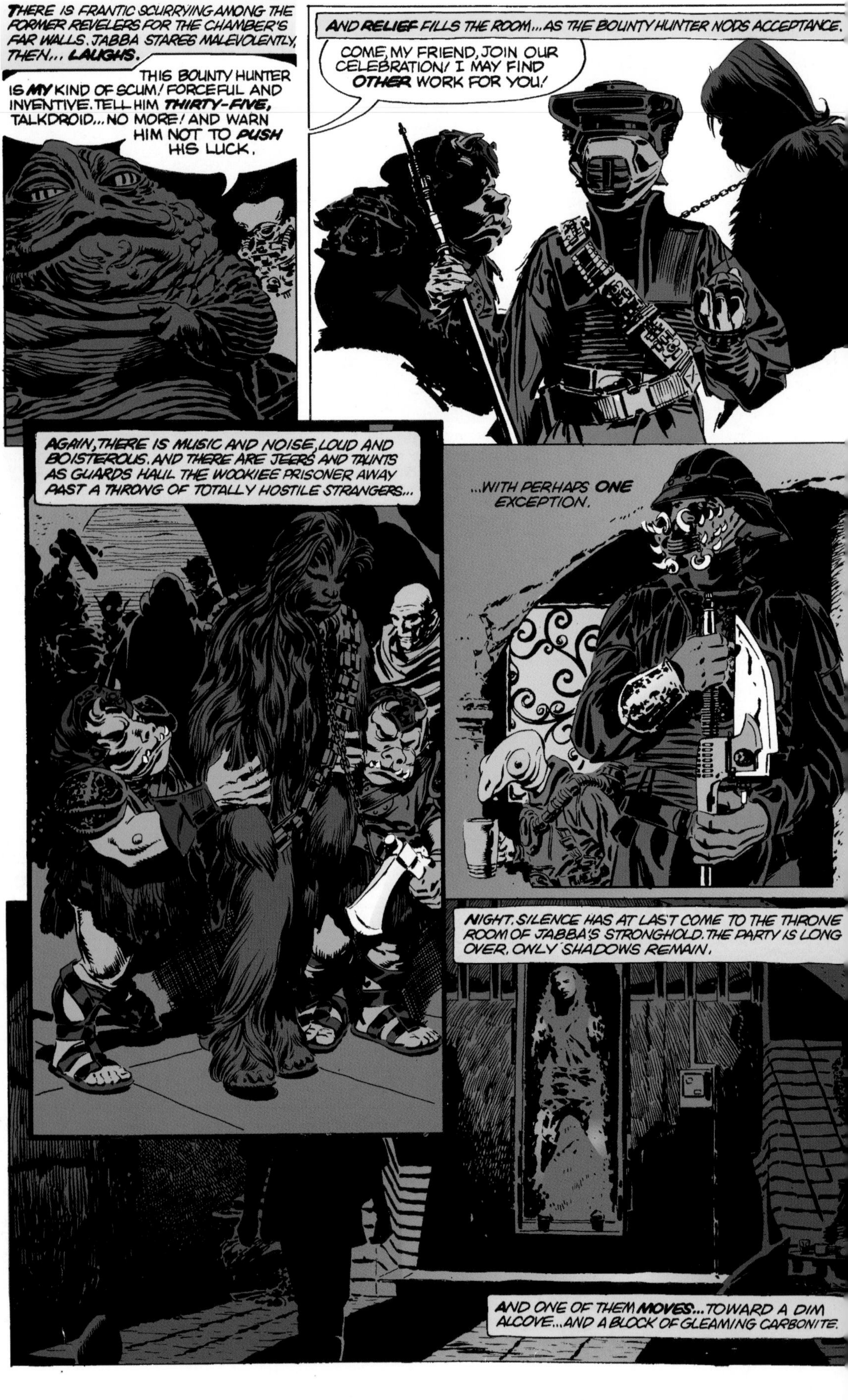
THERE IS FRANTIC SCURRYING AMONG THE FORMER REVELERS FOR THE CHAMBER'S FAR WALLS. JABBA STARES MALEVOLENTLY, THEN... LAUGHS.
THIS BOUNTY HUNTER IS MY KIND OF SCUM! FORCEFUL AND INVENTIVE. TELL HIM THIRTY-FIVE, TALKDROID... NO MORE! AND WARN HIM NOT TO PUSH HIS LUCK.
AND RELIEF FILLS THE ROOM... AS THE BOUNTY HUNTER NODS ACCEPTANCE.
COME, MY FRIEND, JOIN OUR CELEBRATION! I MAY FIND OTHER WORK FOR YOU!
AGAIN, THERE IS MUSIC AND NOISE, LOUD AND BOISTEROUS. AND THERE ARE JEERS AND TAUNTS AS GUARDS HAUL THE WOOKIEE PRISONER AWAY PAST A THRONG OF TOTALLY HOSTILE STRANGERS...
...WITH PERHAPS ONE EXCEPTION.
NIGHT. SILENCE HAS AT LAST COME TO THE THRONE ROOM OF JABBA'S STRONGHOLD. THE PARTY IS LONG OVER. ONLY SHADOWS REMAIN.
AND ONE OF THEM MOVES... TOWARD A DIM ALCOVE... AND A BLOCK OF GLEAMING CARBONITE.

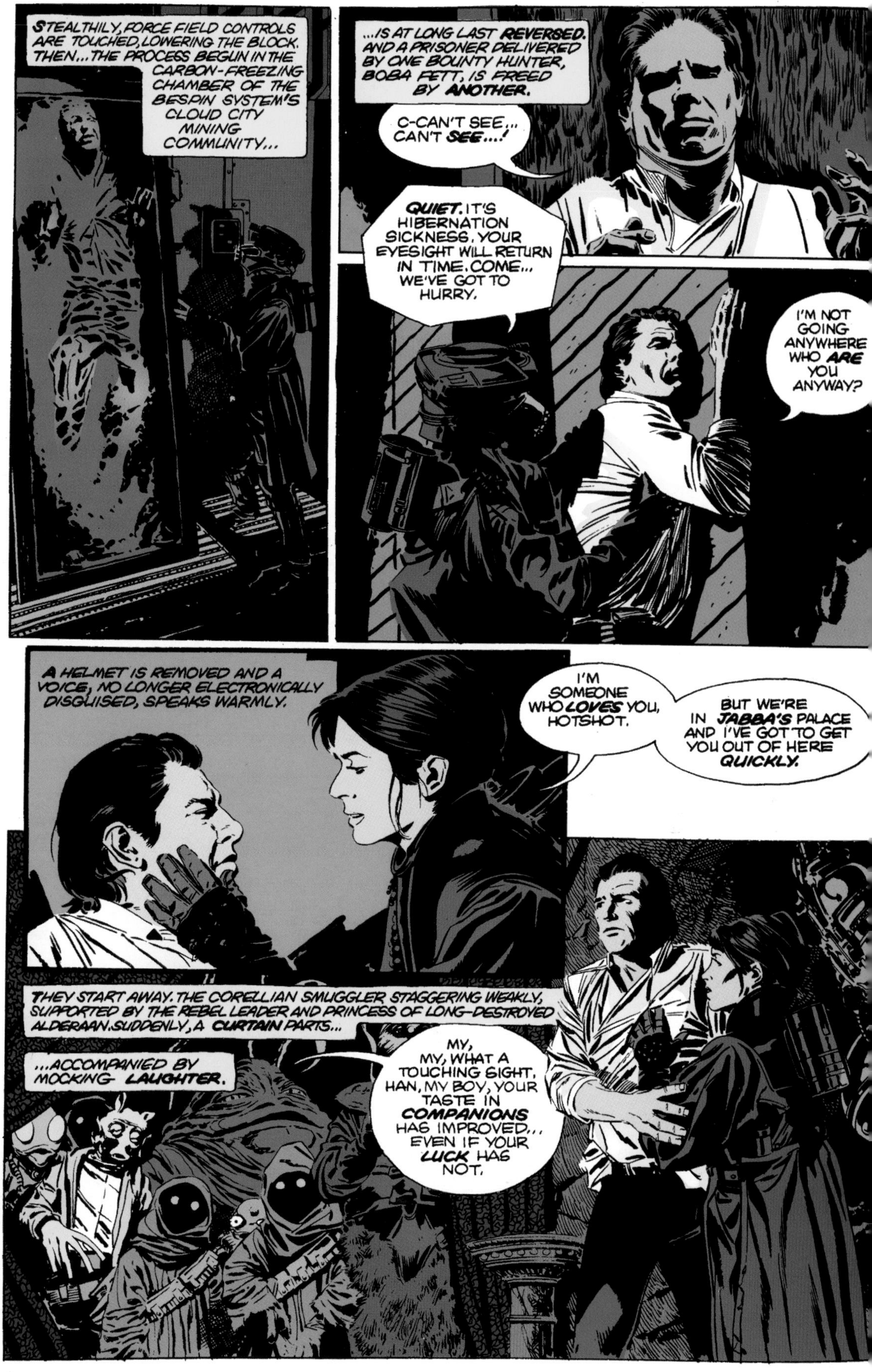
STEALTHILY, FORCE FIELD CONTROLS ARE TOUCHED, LOWERING THE BLOCK. THEN... THE PROCESS BEGUN IN THE CARBON-FREEZING CHAMBER OF THE BESPIN SYSTEM'S CLOUD CITY MINING COMMUNITY...
...IS AT LONG LAST REVERSED. AND A PRISONER DELIVERED BY ONE BOUNTY HUNTER, BOBA FETT, IS FREED BY ANOTHER.
C-CAN'T SEE... CAN'T SEE...!
QUIET. IT'S HIBERNATION SICKNESS. YOUR EYESIGHT WILL RETURN IN TIME. COME... WE'VE GOT TO HURRY.
I'M NOT GOING ANYWHERE WHO ARE YOU ANYWAY?
A HELMET IS REMOVED AND A VOICE, NO LONGER ELECTRONICALLY DISGUISED, SPEAKS WARMLY.
I'M SOMEONE WHO LOVES YOU, HOTSHOT.
BUT WE'RE IN JABBA'S PALACE AND I'VE GOT TO GET YOU OUT OF HERE QUICKLY.
THEY START AWAY. THE CORELLIAN SMUGGLER STAGGERING WEAKLY, SUPPORTED BY THE REBEL LEADER AND PRINCESS OF LONG-DESTROYED ALDERAAN. SUDDENLY, A CURTAIN PARTS...
...ACCOMPANIED BY MOCKING LAUGHTER.
MY, MY, WHAT A TOUCHING SIGHT. HAN, MY BOY, YOUR TASTE IN COMPANIONS HAS IMPROVED... EVEN IF YOUR LUCK HAS NOT.

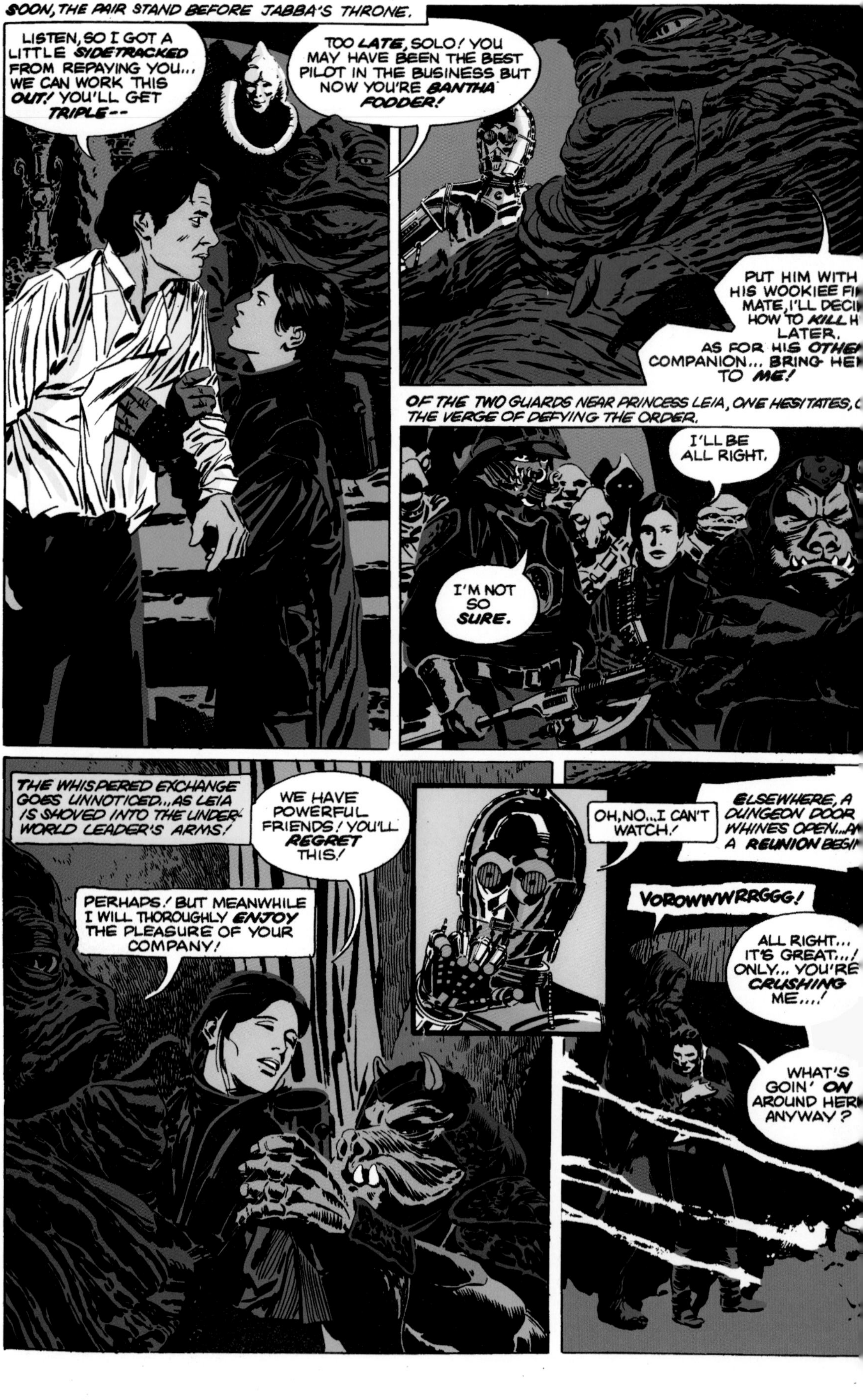

SOON, THE PAIR STAND BEFORE JABBA'S THRONE.
LISTEN, SO I GOT A LITTLE SIDETRACKED FROM REPAYING YOU... WE CAN WORK THIS OUT! YOU'LL GET TRIPLE--
TOO LATE, SOLO! YOU MAY HAVE BEEN THE BEST PILOT IN THE BUSINESS BUT NOW YOU'RE BANTHA FODDER!
PUT HIM WITH HIS WOOKIEE FI MATE, I'LL DECI HOW TO KILL H LATER. AS FOR HIS OTHE COMPANION... BRING HE TO ME!
OF THE TWO GUARDS NEAR PRINCESS LEIA, ONE HESITATES, THE VERGE OF DEFYING THE ORDER.
I'LL BE ALL RIGHT.
I'M NOT SO SURE.
THE WHISPERED EXCHANGE GOES UNNOTICED... AS LEIA IS SHOVED INTO THE UNDER-WORLD LEADER'S ARMS!
WE HAVE POWERFUL FRIENDS! YOU'LL REGRET THIS!
PERHAPS! BUT MEANWHILE I WILL THOROUGHLY ENJOY THE PLEASURE OF YOUR COMPANY!
OH, NO... I CAN'T WATCH!
ELSEWHERE, A DUNGEON DOOR WHINES OPEN... A A REUNION BEGI
VOROWWWRRGGG!
ALL RIGHT... IT'S GREAT...! ONLY... YOU'RE CRUSHING ME....!
WHAT'S GOIN' ON AROUND HER ANYWAY?

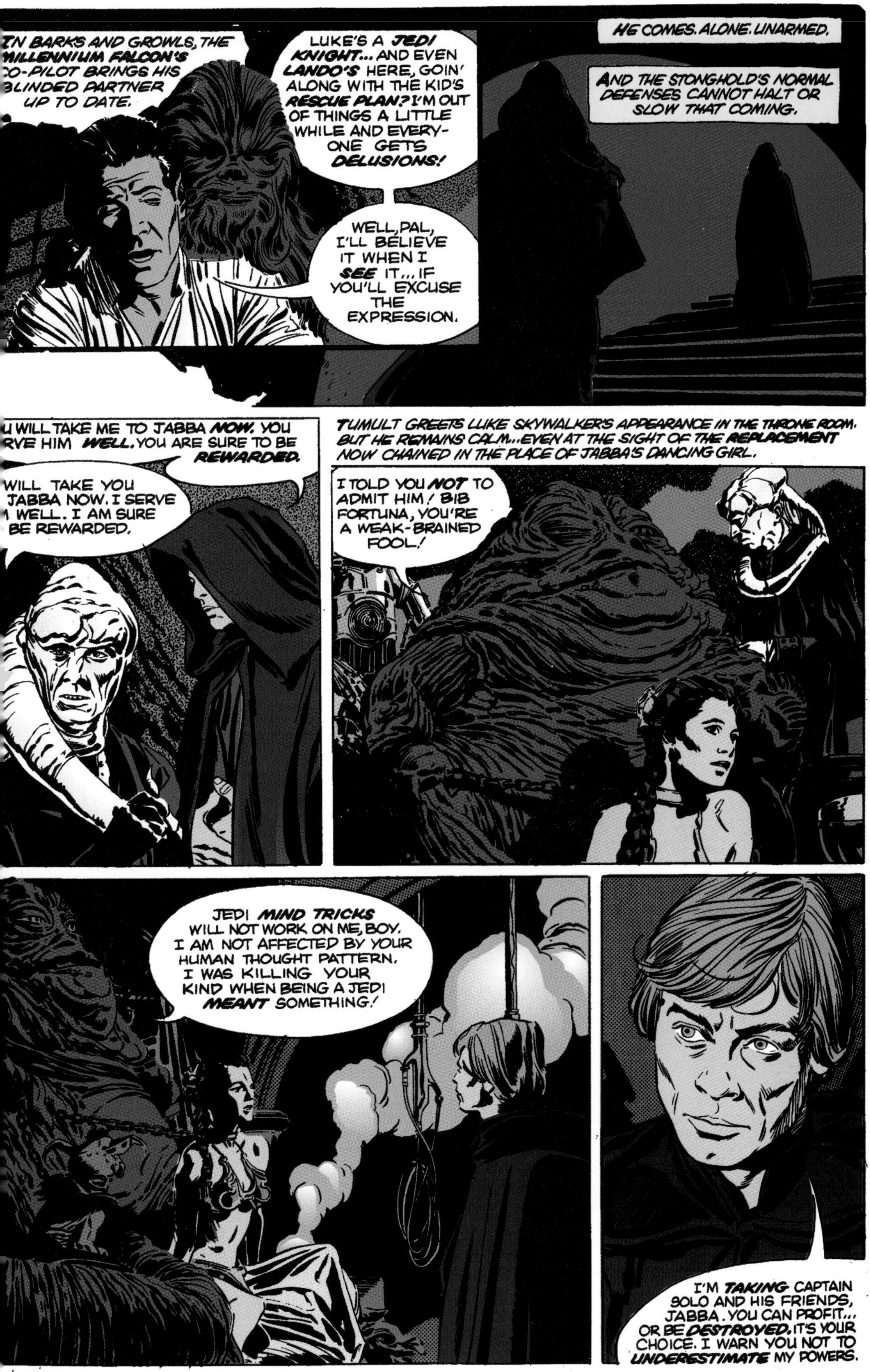
IN BARKS AND GROWLS, THE MILLENNIUM FALCON'S CO-PILOT BRINGS HIS BLINDED PARTNER UP TO DATE.
LUKE'S A JEDI KNIGHT... AND EVEN LANDO'S HERE, GOIN' ALONG WITH THE KID'S RESCUE PLAN? I'M OUT OF THINGS A LITTLE WHILE AND EVERY-ONE GETS DELUSIONS!
WELL, PAL, I'LL BELIEVE IT WHEN I SEE IT... IF YOU'LL EXCUSE THE EXPRESSION.
HE COMES. ALONE. UNARMED.
AND THE STONGHOLD'S NORMAL DEFENSES CANNOT HALT OR SLOW THAT COMING.
U WILL TAKE ME TO JABBA NOW. YOU RVE HIM WELL. YOU ARE SURE TO BE REWARDED.
WILL TAKE YOU JABBA NOW. I SERVE WELL. I AM SURE BE REWARDED.
TUMULT GREETS LUKE SKYWALKER'S APPEARANCE IN THE THRONE ROOM. BUT HE REMAINS CALM... EVEN AT THE SIGHT OF THE REPLACEMENT NOW CHAINED IN THE PLACE OF JABBA'S DANCING GIRL.
I TOLD YOU NOT TO ADMIT HIM! BIB FORTUNA, YOU'RE A WEAK-BRAINED FOOL!
JEDI MIND TRICKS WILL NOT WORK ON ME, BOY. I AM NOT AFFECTED BY YOUR HUMAN THOUGHT PATTERN. I WAS KILLING YOUR KIND WHEN BEING A JEDI MEANT SOMETHING!
I'M TAKING CAPTAIN SOLO AND HIS FRIENDS, JABBA. YOU CAN PROFIT... OR BE DESTROYED. IT'S YOUR CHOICE. I WARN YOU NOT TO UNDERESTIMATE MY POWERS.

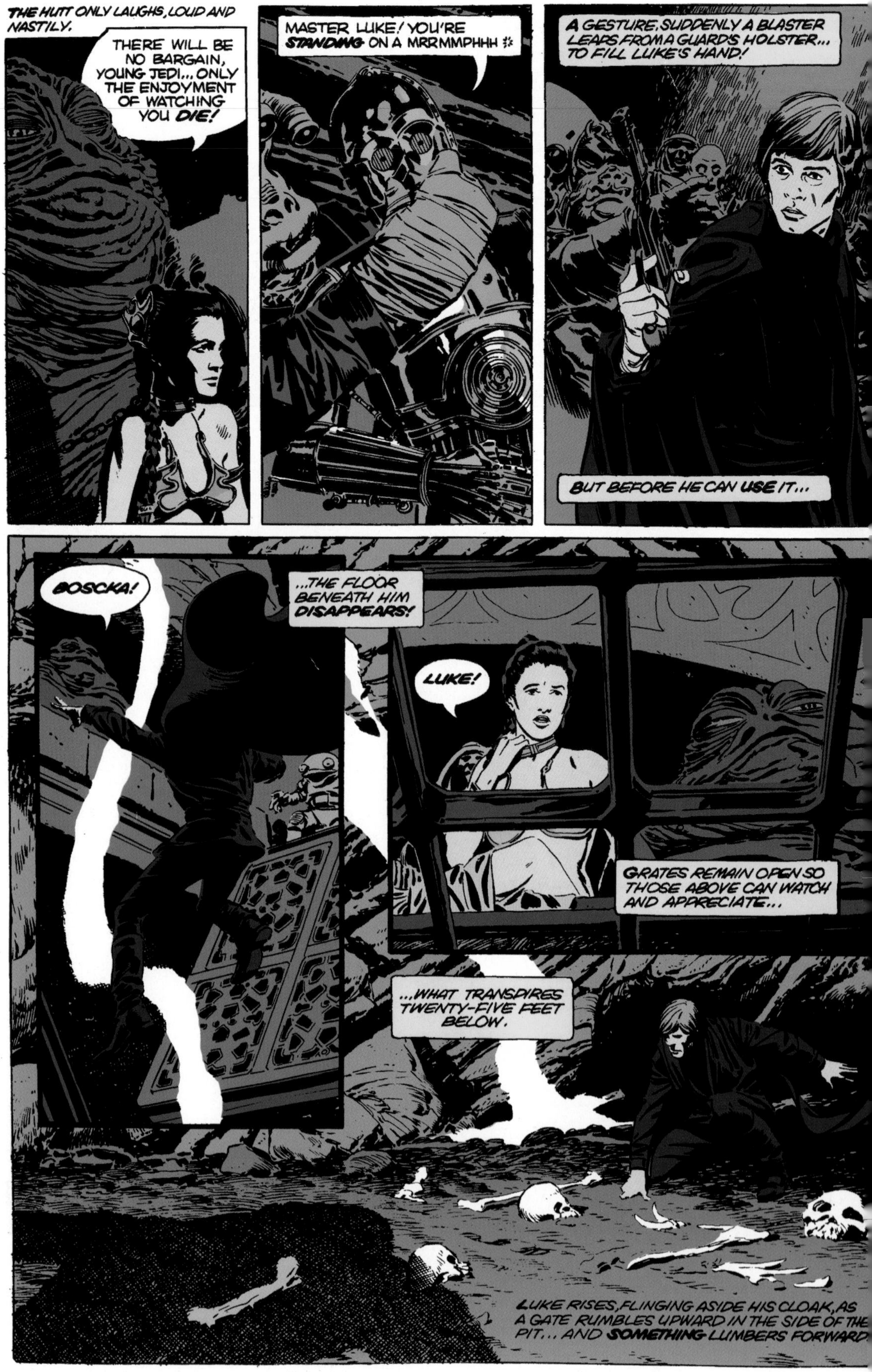

THE HUTT ONLY LAUGHS, LOUD AND NASTILY.
THERE WILL BE NO BARGAIN, YOUNG JEDI... ONLY THE ENJOYMENT OF WATCHING YOU DIE!
MASTER LUKE! YOU'RE STANDING ON A MRRMMPHHH!
A GESTURE. SUDDENLY A BLASTER LEAPS FROM A GUARD'S HOLSTER... TO FILL LUKE'S HAND!
BUT BEFORE HE CAN USE IT...
BOSCKA!
...THE FLOOR BENEATH HIM DISAPPEARS!
LUKE!
GRATES REMAIN OPEN SO THOSE ABOVE CAN WATCH AND APPRECIATE...
...WHAT TRANSPIRES TWENTY-FIVE FEET BELOW.
LUKE RISES, FLINGING ASIDE HIS CLOAK, AS A GATE RUMBLES UPWARD IN THE SIDE OF THE PIT... AND SOMETHING LUMBERS FORWARD!

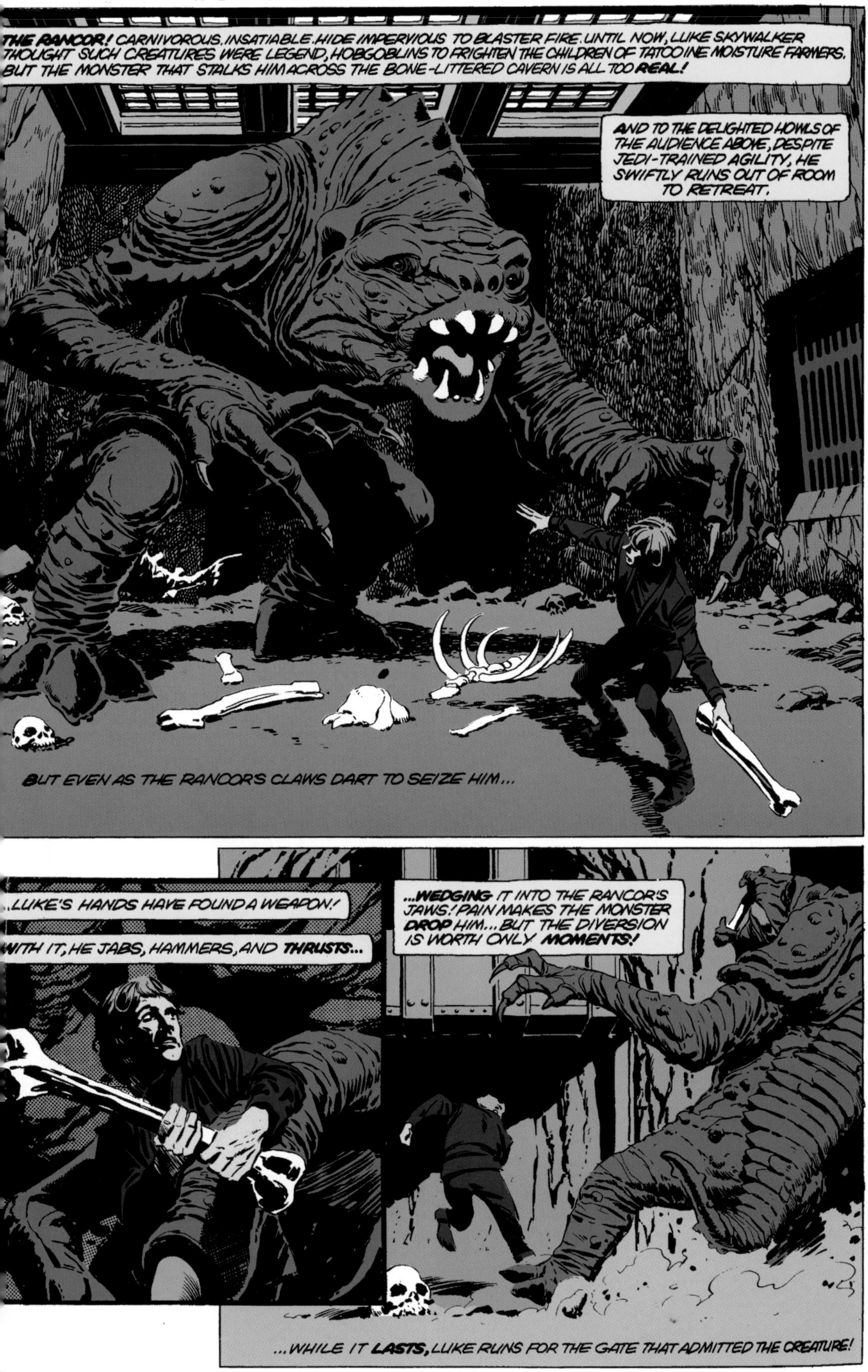
THE RANCOR! CARNIVOROUS. INSATIABLE. HIDE IMPERVIOUS TO BLASTER FIRE. UNTIL NOW, LUKE SKYWALKER THOUGHT SUCH CREATURES WERE LEGEND, HOBGOBLINS TO FRIGHTEN THE CHILDREN OF TATOOINE MOISTURE FARMERS. BUT THE MONSTER THAT STALKS HIM ACROSS THE BONE-LITTERED CAVERN IS ALL TOO REAL!
AND TO THE DELIGHTED HOWLS OF THE AUDIENCE ABOVE, DESPITE JEDI-TRAINED AGILITY, HE SWIFTLY RUNS OUT OF ROOM TO RETREAT.
BUT EVEN AS THE RANCOR'S CLAWS DART TO SEIZE HIM...
...LUKE'S HANDS HAVE FOUND A WEAPON!
WITH IT, HE JABS, HAMMERS, AND THRUSTS...
...WEDGING IT INTO THE RANCOR'S JAWS! PAIN MAKES THE MONSTER DROP HIM... BUT THE DIVERSION IS WORTH ONLY MOMENTS!
...WHILE IT LASTS, LUKE RUNS FOR THE GATE THAT ADMITTED THE CREATURE!

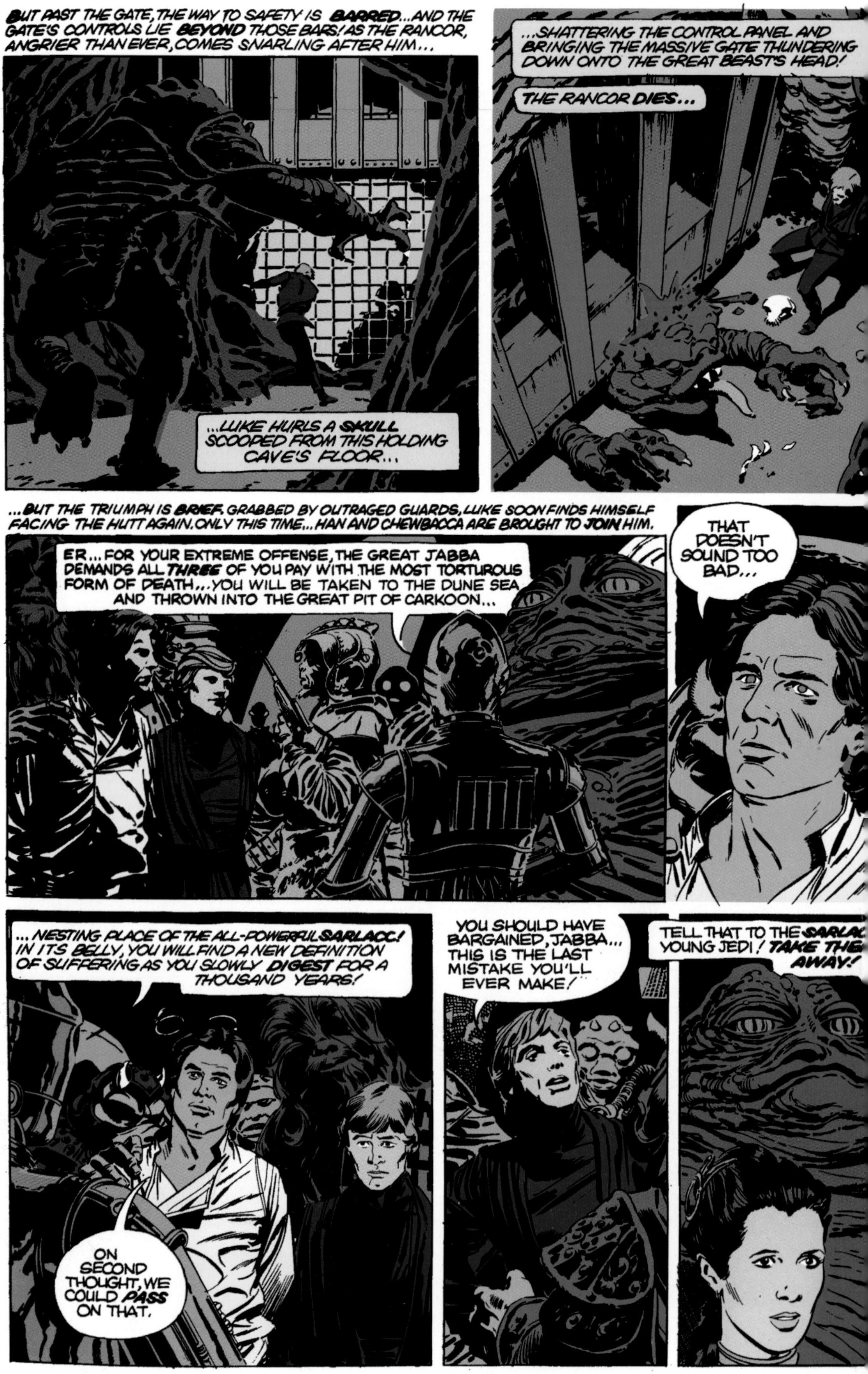
BUT PAST THE GATE, THE WAY TO SAFETY IS BARRED...AND THE GATE'S CONTROLS LIE BEYOND THOSE BARS! AS THE RANCOR, ANGRIER THAN EVER, COMES SNARLING AFTER HIM...
...LUKE HURLS A SKULL SCOOPED FROM THIS HOLDING CAVE'S FLOOR...
...SHATTERING THE CONTROL PANEL AND BRINGING THE MASSIVE GATE THUNDERING DOWN ONTO THE GREAT BEAST'S HEAD!
THE RANCOR DIES...
...BUT THE TRIUMPH IS BRIEF. GRABBED BY OUTRAGED GUARDS, LUKE SOON FINDS HIMSELF FACING THE HUTT AGAIN. ONLY THIS TIME... HAN AND CHEWBACCA ARE BROUGHT TO JOIN HIM.
ER... FOR YOUR EXTREME OFFENSE, THE GREAT JABBA DEMANDS ALL THREE OF YOU PAY WITH THE MOST TORTUROUS FORM OF DEATH... YOU WILL BE TAKEN TO THE DUNE SEA AND THROWN INTO THE GREAT PIT OF CARKOON...
THAT DOESN'T SOUND TOO BAD...
...NESTING PLACE OF THE ALL-POWERFUL SARLACC! IN ITS BELLY, YOU WILL FIND A NEW DEFINITION OF SUFFERING AS YOU SLOWLY DIGEST FOR A THOUSAND YEARS!
ON SECOND THOUGHT, WE COULD PASS ON THAT.
YOU SHOULD HAVE BARGAINED, JABBA... THIS IS THE LAST MISTAKE YOU'LL EVER MAKE!
TELL THAT TO THE SARLAC YOUNG JEDI! TAKE THE AWAY!

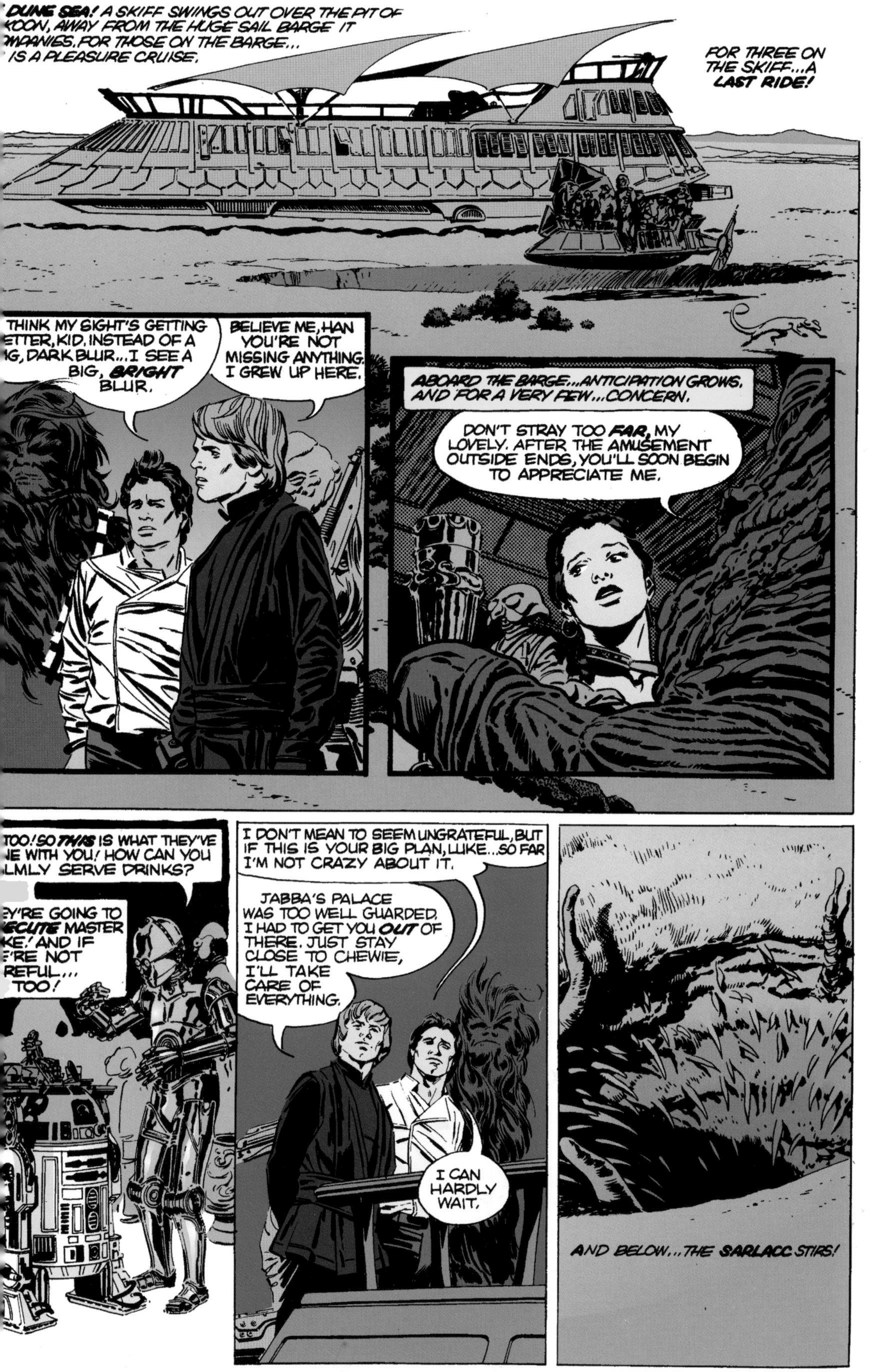
DUNE SEA! A SKIFF SWINGS OUT OVER THE PIT OF
KOON, AWAY FROM THE HUGE SAIL BARGE IT
MPANIES. FOR THOSE ON THE BARGE...
IS A PLEASURE CRUISE.
FOR THREE ON THE SKIFF... A LAST RIDE!
THINK MY SIGHT'S GETTING
ETTER, KID, INSTEAD OF A
IG, DARK BLUR... I SEE A
BIG, BRIGHT BLUR.
BELIEVE ME, HAN YOU'RE NOT MISSING ANYTHING. I GREW UP HERE.
ABOARD THE BARGE... ANTICIPATION GROWS. AND FOR A VERY FEW... CONCERN.
DON'T STRAY TOO FAR, MY LOVELY. AFTER THE AMUSEMENT OUTSIDE ENDS, YOU'LL SOON BEGIN TO APPRECIATE ME.
TOO! SO THIS IS WHAT THEY'VE
NE WITH YOU! HOW CAN YOU
LMLY SERVE DRINKS?
EY'RE GOING TO
ECUTE MASTER
KE! AND IF
E'RE NOT
REFUL...
TOO!
I DON'T MEAN TO SEEM UNGRATEFUL, BUT IF THIS IS YOUR BIG PLAN, LUKE... SO FAR I'M NOT CRAZY ABOUT IT.
JABBA'S PALACE WAS TOO WELL GUARDED. I HAD TO GET YOU OUT OF THERE. JUST STAY CLOSE TO CHEWIE, I'LL TAKE CARE OF EVERYTHING.
I CAN HARDLY WAIT.
AND BELOW... THE SARLACC STIRS!

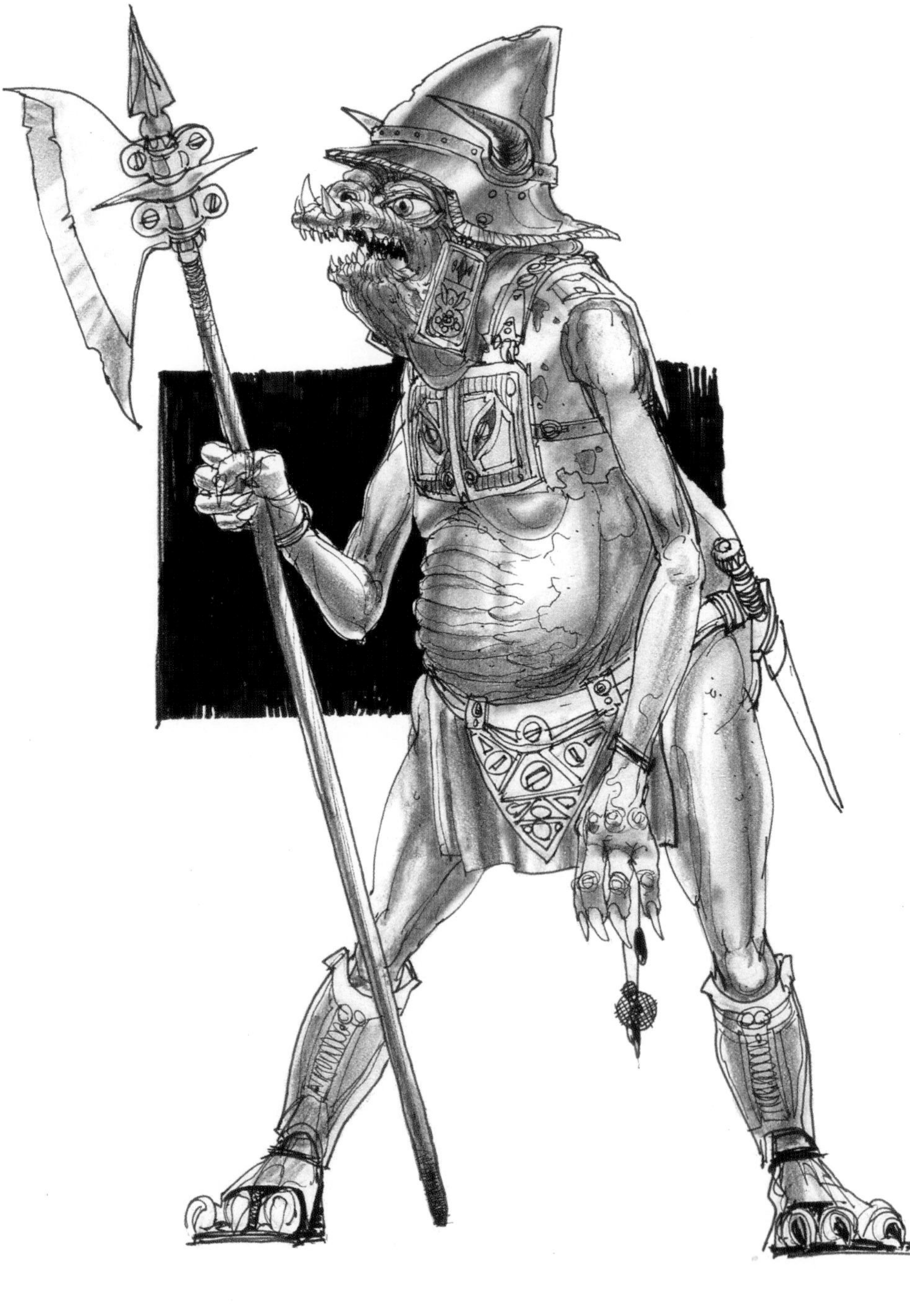

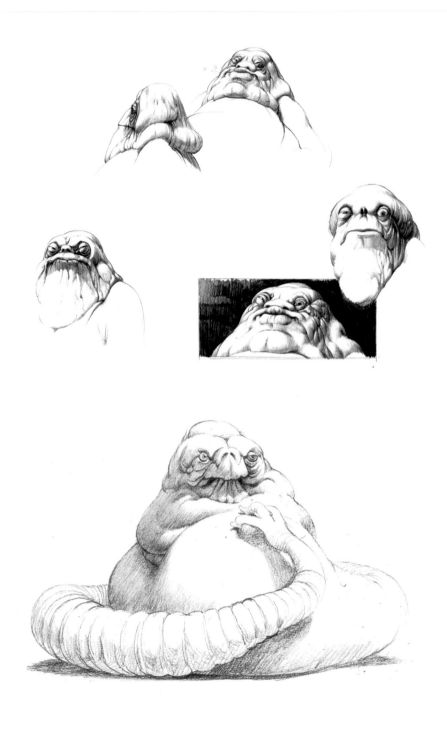

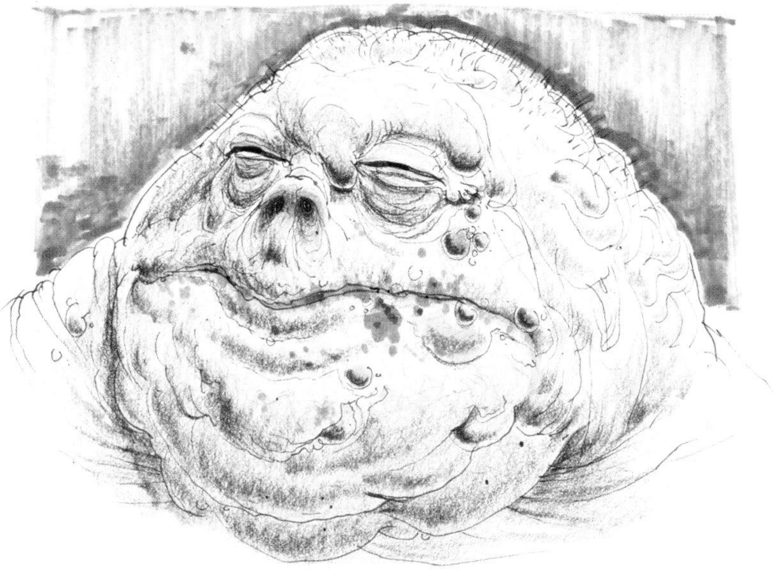

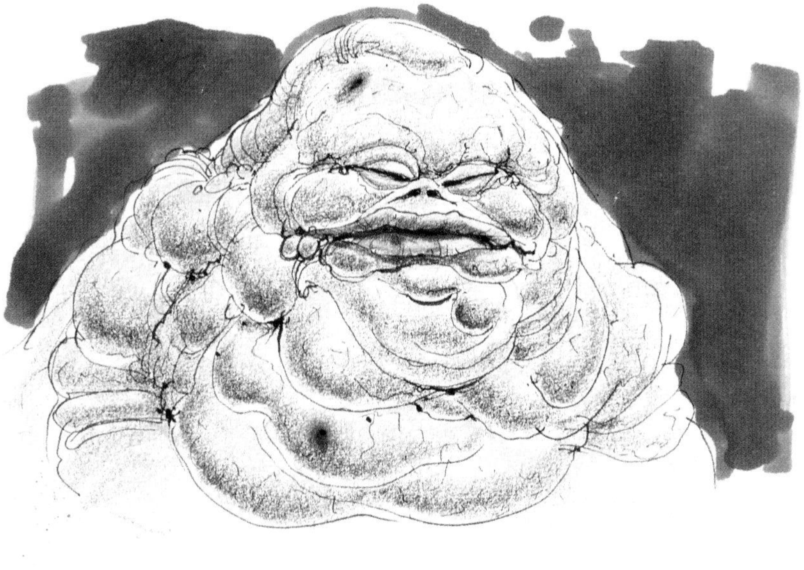

FINES
5¢ PER DAY
FOR
OVERDUE BOOKS